BONE DOG

Eric Rohmann

Roaring Brook Press — New York

To one Larry and two Scotts—thanks for looking closely

Copyright © 2011 by Eric Rohmann
Published by Roaring Brook Press
Roaring Brook Press is a division of Holtzbrinck Publishing Holdings Limited Partnership
175 Fifth Avenue, New York, New York 10010
mackids.com

Library of Congress Cataloging-in-Publication Data

Rohmann, Eric.
    Bone dog / Eric Rohmann. — 1st ed.
        p.   cm.
    Summary: Although devastated when his pet dog dies, a young boy goes trick-or-treating
and receives a timely visit from an old friend during a scary encounter with graveyard skeletons.
    ISBN 978-1-59643-150-8
    [1. Dogs—Fiction. 2. Death—Fiction. 3. Skeleton—Fiction. 4. Halloween—Fiction.] I. Title.
PZ7.R6413Bo 2011
[E]—dc22

                                                                                2010045142

Roaring Brook Press books are available for special promotions and premiums.
For details contact: Director of Special Markets, Holtzbrinck Publishers.

First edition 2011
Book design by Andrew Arnold
Printed in March 2011 in China by Toppan Leefung Printing Ltd., Dongguan City, Guangdong Province

1 3 5 7 9 10 8 6 4 2

Ella and Gus had been friends for a long, long time.

One night Ella said, "I'm an old dog and won't be around much longer. But no matter what happens, I'll always be with you."

For a long while they sat together in the moonlight. Then Ella said, "A promise made under a full moon cannot be broken."

After Ella was gone, Gus didn't feel like leaving the house. But he did.

He didn't want to do his chores. But he did.

And when Halloween came around,
Gus didn't feel like trick-or-treating.

But he pulled on his costume and
trudged out the door.

When the night grew dark and his bag grew heavy, Gus started home.

Past the school, around the pond, and through the graveyard . . .

The wind moaned.

The clouds swallowed the moon.

Gus was surrounded.

"Come along now," said a skeleton. "It's Halloween and you know what that means."

"What *does* it mean?" asked Gus.

"Numbskull," snorted another skeleton.

Then they all danced and sang out, "We shriek and growl, screech and swoon, hiss and howl, 'neath the blood red moon!

"You know . . . skeleton stuff."

"But I'm not a skeleton"
Gus said. "I'm a boy."

"A boy!"

"And he's alive!"

"And you know what that means?"

"Bone appétit!!"

They lunged at Gus.

"You've got guts kid . . . but not for long!"

Just then, the wind calmed and the moon
broke shimmering from the clouds.

The skeletons whirled.

"Ella!" cried Gus.

"A bone dog?" cried the skeletons.

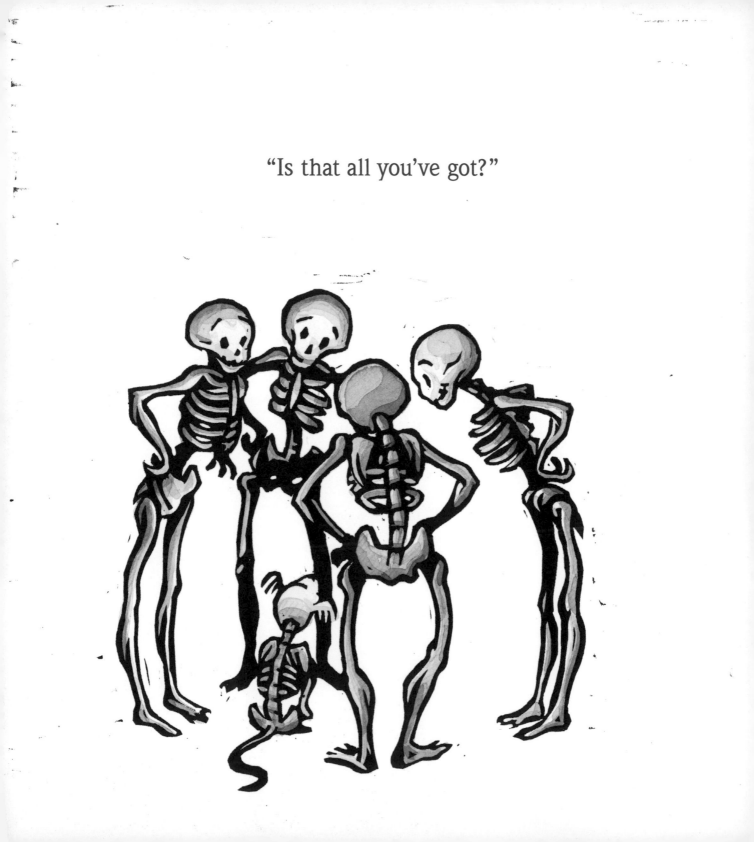

"Well, tickle my ribs, why would *we* be afraid of a bone dog?"

Ella barked and growled. It gave Gus an idea.

He joined in barking and growling. Together, with all their might and at the top of their voices, boy and dog howled into the night.

A moment later, an answer came from the distance.
The skeletons stopped dead in their tracks.

"Woof?"

Afterwards, Gus and Ella sat together in the moonlight. Gus asked, "Will I see you again?"

"A promise made under a full moon cannot be broken," said Ella.

With that she disappeared into the night.

And Gus picked up his bag and headed for home.